My Eyes, His Heart

ENCOUNTERS
OF A
MEDICAL
MISSIONARY

W. "Ted" Kuhn, M.D.

WINEPRESS **WP** PUBLISHING

Packaged by WinePress Publishing, PO Box 428, Enumclaw, WA 98022. The views expressed or implied in this work do not necessarily reflect those of WinePress Publishing. The author(s) is ultimately responsible for the design, content, and editorial accuracy of this work.

Scriptures marked NIV are taken from the Holy Bible, New International Version, Copyright © 1973, 1978, 1984 by the International Bible Society. Used by permission of Zondervan Publishing House. The "NIV" and "New International Version" trademarks are registered in the United States Patent and Trademark Office by International Bible Society.

Scriptures marked RSV are taken from the Revised Standard Version of the Bible. Copyright © 1946, 1952, 1971 by the Division of Christian Education of the National Council of the Churches of Christ in the U.S.A. Used by permission.

ISBN 1-57921-479-7

Library of Congress Catalog Card Number: 2002107012

To my wife, Sharon. You are the love of my life; my co-worker, fellow physician, mother of our precious covenant children, missionary, prayer warrior, encourager, help-mate, colleague, and running partner.

I do not cease to give thanks for you, remembering you in my prayers, that the God of our Lord Jesus Christ, the Father of glory, may give you a spirit of wisdom and of revelation in the knowledge of him, having the eyes of your heart enlightened, that you may know what is the hope to which he has called you . . .
—Ephesians 1:16–18, RSV

I WOULD LIKE TO THANK
my daughter, Lydia, for many of the excellent photos included in this
book. You have an "eye" for His heart.

Contents

Photos

All photos used with permission of photographer.

Preface

I have had the unique privilege over the years to travel to many parts of the world, to meet and to provide medical care for some of the poorest and most needy people on the face of the planet. My travels have taken me from my home, south to the Caribbean, Central America, and South America, and across the Atlantic and Pacific Oceans to Africa, the Middle East, the Subcontinent, and Asia. *My Eyes, His Heart* is a collection of short stories about the people I have met during those travels. If you have eyes to see, everyone is a story. These short stories portray the lives of people as I experienced them. Yes, there really is a widow with a headache in the slums of Manila. And yes, there really is (was) a Roberto, Noella, Archona, and Damaris. There is a slum called Belén and a harlot of Belén. There is a dying room in Manila. And there really is a broken china teacup.

Years ago I was challenged to ask God to break my heart with the things that break His heart. As I travel I ask God to allow me to see people and circumstances as He sees them. To see them through His eyes and with His heart. To think His thoughts after Him. The stories in *My Eyes, His Heart* are "word pictures" and are my attempt to see others the way God would have me see them—all unique, all interesting, all made in His image, and all very precious in His sight.

—*Ted Kuhn, M.D.*
Sparta, N.C.

Tree with Vultures

Roberto

—✐—

She sat quietly in a line on the bench waiting for her turn to see the doctor. The late-afternoon light was fading in the small church, now makeshift clinic. The temperature was dropping and several team members reached for coats and jackets. It was becoming hard to see with the one dangling light bulb suspended from a wire. She sat quietly, patiently. She looked like all the others. A ragged red sweater, a wide wool skirt, and plastic slippers. She had long, black, braided hair streaked with white strands under her black bowler hat. Her face tanned from the high mountain sun. Her hands cracked from the dry air and the hard work of many years. The only thing that distinguished her from the others was a brown, wool blanket neatly folded on her lap.

"I want to trade this," she said holding out the blanket. Philip tried to explain that the medicine was free. There was no need to give us the precious blanket. No, she insisted. My son made this blanket. I want to trade this blanket for my son.

Her son, Roberto, had been ill for several years. Before, she explained, he had been a normal boy. Several years ago he began acting strangely. He wandered the entire day sitting in the garbage piles of Huancavelica. He scrounged for food with the dogs in the trash and lost his clothes. He walked around naked in the dirt streets. Some days he would be gone all day. Other days he just sat and stared, sometimes not speaking the entire day. "I will give this to you," she said once again, holding out the blanket to Philip, "just give me back my son."

The next day we searched the hillside village. At first we could not find him. Then we spotted him following us at a distance. He had been watching us quietly from behind. Roberto squatted against the wall of a mud house. He stared wide-eyed at us, his mother quietly comforting in Quechua. He was a young man of about eighteen, thin and gaunt. His angular face was tight from lack of food. He wore a pair of brown shorts torn at the waist and leg, exposing him. He wore no shirt or shoes. His body covered with dirt, his skin dry and cracked, seemingly impervious to the cold. His black hair uncombed and a short stubble of beard on his chin, like that of an unshaven high school boy. At first we thought he might welcome us. Then, like a stray dog desiring to be petted but who runs away in confusion and fear, he turned and withdrew. Surprisingly, he walked behind us and followed us back to the clinic. His mother persuaded him to speak with us. Yes, he heard and saw things other people did not see and hear. Sometimes the dead spoke to him and he saw visions. Sometimes these visions frightened him. He found peace sitting in the trash piles. The voices did not torment him there.

Pastor Luis prayed for Roberto, speaking to him softly, gently and lovingly. I could not understand the words, but the meaning was clear. Jesus was the protector. The author of the universe could protect him from the frightful voices and visions. Jesus has power over the seen and the unseen, that which exists to touch and that which exists only in our minds. He has the keys to Heaven and Hell and has the power to unlock the darkness of our hearts.

Pastor Luis promised that the small Quechua congregation would pray for his recovery, for his peace. We left a month's supply of an anti-psychotic medication with his mother along with instructions on how to adjust the dosage. We would purchase more in Lima and send it to her by Pastor Luis. She understood.

Over a year has come and gone. Several teams have visited Huancavelica. No one has seen or heard from Roberto. Pastor Luis moved from the Huancavelica church to another church. Neither Roberto nor his mother can be found.

The story of Roberto remains unfinished, like thousands of stories in hundreds of cities. I dream that maybe the story has a wonderful ending. Perhaps Roberto was delivered from his demons by the prayers of the faithful and lives on a small potato farm with his mother just outside the city. Or maybe the story has a tragic ending. Perhaps he died, frozen to death on the trash heaps of Huancavelica, tormented by voices and visions. His mother distraught, moved away. Only God knows for sure.

Shakespeare wrote that life is a comedy to those who think, and a tragedy to those who feel. Nevertheless, I continue to pray that God will break my heart with the things that break His heart. I have had my heart broken often. Roberto breaks my heart. I find my thoughts often going back to Huancavelica, to the day I first met him squatting against a mud wall. A vision of his face and his tattered clothes remains with me these many days. His unfinished story burdens my heart.

But on display, at Philip's house, in a subdivision of Augusta, Georgia, there sits folded a brown woolen blanket. A testimony to a mother's love, a physician's burden, a pastor's prayer, and God's all encompassing grace, a silent witness to a sacrifice made in exchange for a young man's life

Huancavelica, Peru

The Widow's Headache

She wore a pair of broken plastic glasses with wire securing the earpieces. Thus the glasses sat at a peculiar angle on her nose, making her face appear slanted. The lenses were old and badly scratched, seemingly opalescent; almost the color of her white hair set against her brown, wrinkled face. I wondered how she could see. She listed her age as sixty-five. Surely a grandmother by now. She wore an old but clean smock. One simple little lady among a multitude of Manila's poor slum dwellers. I immediately liked her. She was comfortable to be around, neat and generous with her smile. She had dressed in her best to come see the doctor. She sat close to me and leaned forward when she spoke.

"I have a headache", she said. "It comes every morning and stays all day. It gets better in the evening then returns the next morning after I get up." It has been bothering me for about three years. "Every day?" I asked. "Every day," she replied.

"What about Saturdays, Sundays and days off?" "No, every day," she replied. "And on holidays when you don't work?" "I work every day," she replied. "What about Christmas and New Year's?" "No, I work those days as well." This little grandmother assured me that she worked at least twelve hours a day every day of the

13

year and had been doing so for years. "What kind of work do you do?" I naively asked.

"I pick broken glass out of the garbage," she replied. She lived in the slums surrounding the small church that we had converted into a clinic. A precious light in the midst of millions of the poor and displaced. No family, a widow living alone. She explained that there was a landfill behind where she lived near some industry. She sorted broken glass from the garbage. The glass could be sold. If she did not gather glass, she did not eat. Simple economics. Broken glass equals food and life.

I wanted to see for myself. There were narrow planks forming a walkway into the slum area where she lived. The boards provided a shaky passage over the black water and refuse beneath the slum village. The boards sagged under my weight. The "houses" were the size of an appliance box, perhaps the size of an American washing machine or refrigerator. Entire families lived in these "houses" of old packing crates and tin. I could easily touch several "houses" on both sides of the planks with my arms extended. One upon the other, row upon row. The population of an entire city in the space of one block. There were small charcoal fires next to the planks—an outdoor kitchen and sewer all in one.

Despite the cramped living, squalid conditions and pervasive smell, the people were happy to see me. They smiled and waved approvingly as I held on to each house, trying not to slip from the narrow planks into the oil-black water. Several waved me into their homes desiring to visit. The widow's house was on the second level, sitting on top of another small makeshift home. It was about four feet high, just high enough to crawl in on your knees. This small packing crate of a home was neat and clean, just like my patient. A plant hung outside in the afternoon sun for decoration and a single blanket was neatly folded at one corner. A tiny place to belong to, a place to call home.

I emerged from the darkness of the plank streets on the other side of the squatter village into the late afternoon sun. Another shaky bridge over a stagnant stream separated the village from a decaying industrial area. Beyond this was a row of trucks and a garbage dump. Fires belched back acrid smoke, and the smell of burning trash and rubber filled the air. The smell assaulted me, and my eyes teared from the smoke. My skin pricked with dirt and grime. Several older women bent over the garbage scrounging for small treasures that could be exchanged for food. Now I understood. I had traveled 13,000 miles to find the source of a widow's headache. The same garbage pile that brought food and life also brought sickness and death.

Last night when I slipped into the clean sheets of my bed, the same disquieting vision appeared—an old woman bending over a smoking garbage pile. Her hand shields her head, yet gives no relief. She breathes the black air that offers life, but life with suffering. Half a world separating us, yet so close I can touch her broken glasses. My day spent, her day beginning. My stomach full, hers empty. My family surrounds me, she is alone.

I know that eternity is much longer than the life we now lead. And I know that we are but sojourners in this world. I know that we will live surrounded by the beauty of the Bridegroom and we will join heavenly choirs before the throne of God Almighty. I know that wars will cease. There will be no more hunger or pain. And God Himself will be the husband to the widow. But in all fairness, why is her life now so hard?

There is a biblical injunction that we honor widows, treat older women as mothers, and provide for those in need. But what if the local church is so poor that they cannot feed themselves? Are they still not responsible for the widow? Are we not responsible? Is she not part of the body of Christ? Am I not part of that same body? Could her hunger be due in part to me? Lying here in bed, waiting for sleep to come, yet somehow seeing her, I find myself without excuse.

Photo by Lydia Kuhn

Slums of Manila

Living in a Box
Slums of Manila

Child, Slums of Manila

Managua

In the humid, still air of the early morning, I can look out of my hotel balcony at the magnificent view of Managua below. The hotel is built on the side of an inactive volcano and gives me a clear view of the city and Lago de Managua, the enormous lake beyond. I can see mountain ranges on the other side of the lake, including at least two active volcanoes. A pencil line of smoke billows from both their craters. The panorama is breathtaking.

Far below me the city is coming alive. Cars, buses, and people bustle along the roads to work. On the road up the mountain, school children dressed in blue and white uniforms hold hands for their trek up the mountain to a school behind the hotel. Directly beneath me, in front of the hotel and under the shade of a spreading tree bearing bright, orange flowers, I hear the faint sound of Latino music from the car radio of a taxi. The driver lovingly wipes off the cab with a white towel. A lush tropical green envelops the entire city. The treetops are alive with flowers and with the songs of tropical birds.

The people here are bright and attractive, their smiles spontaneous. They appear relaxed and generous and emanate a cultured beauty. White and brown skins and eyes that flash a curious welcome. I am strangely accepted here in this mix of Central

American humanity. And there is a façade of peace and a sense of well-being.

Yet, nothing could be further from reality. High above the city lava boils to the top of volcanoes that literally encircle Managua. A ring of fire. And from below, geologic plates imperceptibly slip, becoming increasingly unstable. From my window I can see the ruins of a Spanish basilica built in the 1700s still undergoing repair from the last major earthquake, scaffoldings erect. I am uneasy as I ponder my own fate should another earthquake occur. I remember a sign on the door outside my room, "No Es Salida" (no exit). How would I, or could I escape? Would I be entombed in my hotel room, just another body trapped by falling debris in the midst of a city of rubble?

Why would the city founders construct a city surrounded on all sides by volcanoes? And why is this city growing and rebuilding when the very ground is shifting even as they walk to work and school? Why do people appear so unconcerned when destruction is both above and beneath? On this peaceful morning, one thing appears certain, a volcano will eventually erupt and there will be another earthquake. And since the city has grown to perhaps two million, countless lives will be lost in an instant. Looking over the lush tropical green, the reality of it is hard to imagine. It's only a question of time.

Beneath the captivating faces and friendly smiles, there is another cauldron of fire. These are the same people who were locked in the mortal combat of civil war only several years past. A bloody war of torture, massacres, and political executions.

A young woman proudly escorts me through one of the neighborhoods. She is attractive, intelligent, and hospitable. I know from our conversation that she enjoyed privileges during the war and she hints that she was a Sandinista rebel. I cannot help but wonder what this bright, attractive, young woman's role might have been during the fighting. I never ask. Perhaps the past is best left undisturbed.

We walk down a side street toward a Catholic cathedral dating from the 1700s. The sun is hot, the afternoon lazy and sultry. And she is visibly proud of her heritage and of this place. We walk past homes in need of repair. I guess that there must have been fierce fighting along this street. She points to bullet holes in the stucco walls. Some houses are marked with red paint "FSLN" and others are marked with "Sandino".

The road is paved in slippery cobblestone, worn smooth by centuries of traffic. There are vendors with wooden carts along the sidewalk. A woman peeling mangoes throws a bucket of water on the street just yards in front of me. The sound and sight of water splashing on the cobblestone startles me and water runs under my shoes. The water pools in the cracks of the cobblestone and eventually finds its way into a ditch. My guide tells me that there were many executions along this street. I consider that it has not been long since these same cracks were filled with blood. How many died? What were their names? All were someone's father, mother, brother, or sister. How many of those who now smile as I pass by held guns? And what cleverly devised arguments could compel a neighbor to pull a trigger to end the life of a friend? How much spilled blood is enough? Will the water from mangoes ever wash away the stain?

There is a desolation of the soul more profound than volcanoes and earthquakes. A sinister darkness beneath the surface— like hot lava threatening to consume us. We, like Managua, live with the threat of devastation. And we, like the city, live unconcerned, as if judgment will never come. The date and time of the next disaster in Managua is uncertain. But that it will eventually come, is certain. It will take them unaware but not unforewarned. Yes, there is foolishness in Managua, a sense of prosperity in the midst of a ring of fire as destruction draws near. An exit has been provided. Escape freely offered. Nevertheless, few accept. Are we so different?

La Casa de Somoza

Through some quirk of politics, the Managua mansion of former Nicaraguan dictator Somoza now belonged to the United States. All I needed was my American passport for entrance. Dinner was to be with several of my American and Nicaraguan friends. The property was under tight security. Our car was scanned for plastic explosives by some sort of computerized device as we entered the gates. Armed Nicaraguan guards carrying machine guns and grenades surrounded us and checked our identity. The whole property was bordered with cantina wire and guard posts. After we passed security, there was a winding road up to the mansion through gardens and an open grassy area. I was enveloped by a peace and quiet as we approached. The stillness, the first I had known since coming to Nicaragua, was a striking contrast to the commotion of downtown Managua.

We parked on a circular driveway under a majestic tree near the front of the mansion. One of the marine guards relaxed in the swimming pool to the right of the driveway, next to the tennis court. The air was hot but strangely sweet, laced with the fragrance of some tropical flower. The entrance doors were of heavy wood and reminded me of the doors to cathedrals in Central America. The atrium of the house was majestic with winding stairs to the upper level. The floor was made of black and white marble and a chandelier hung in the center. A desk of inlayed polished wood was the centerpiece adorned with fresh tropical flowers. On each side of the atrium, there were hallways, like spokes of a wheel. One hallway led toward the dining area and another to two large lounges, one with a piano and the other with a stage. I could see all Managua from the bay windows of the great room. The lights of Managua, like tiny flashing stars at our feet. What wealth and privilege the original owners must have enjoyed.

I toured several of the rooms while waiting for supper. One great room with an elevated stage had been designed for plays. Behind this was a paneled library, with classic, dark polished wood paneling and bookcases. And there were comfortable overstuffed chairs. Priceless leather bound volumes curiously mixed with paperback American romance novels from the 1950s and 60s. Next to a series of leather law books from Nicaragua was a well-worn Ayn Rand paperback. On one side of the room a billiard table sat in perfect condition. The green felt immaculate and striking against the background of the dark wooden paneling and old leather books.

I was aware that I was in the residence of a former Nicaraguan dictator. Certainly, he used this library and this very billiard table. He had stood here, in this very room. What kind of man could he have been? Did he play with his children beside the billiard table? Is this the very room where he planned his grand political schemes? Did he discuss assassination plots and atrocities in this very spot? Although I stood in his shadow, I sensed no evil. I could hear the chatter of my American and Nicaraguan friends, happy in their fellowship with one another. No, evil does not reside in buildings, or magnificent mansions, but in the hearts and minds of men. Tonight I was here with my Christian friends and we were happy to be together in this beautiful place. The evil is long gone and Christ resides in the hearts of my companions, whose voices I heard in the background. Tonight, Somoza's mansion was Christ's home.

White linen napkins and crystal glasses were set at the dinner table. After my salad I was served savory blackened fish. The vegetables were fresh and sprinkled with tasty spices, and fresh bread and muffins filled the long white table. I turned down the blueberry cheesecake and settled for a cup of dark Nicaraguan coffee. We reclined in our chairs and discussed the war, the church, and business opportunities in Nicaragua. After coffee we embraced and promised to visit. All was well, all at peace. We had a wonderful meal in a grand mansion. We left through the cantina wire and guard posts and the Nicaraguan soldiers bid us good night. "Yet a little while, and the wicked will be no more, though you look well at his place, he will not be there."[1] Tonight, I will sleep. I have sojourned in the mansion of a ruthless dictator and he was not there. His house was filled with laughter, fellowship, and Christian love—and I am at peace.

---

[1] Psalm 37:10 RSV

At the End of Broken Dreams

T he Military Hospital in Managua sits high on the rim of an inactive volcano overlooking the city. It is a massive building. There is fresh red paint on the entrance. Although the buildings are forty to fifty years old and crowded, the facilities seem adequate. I sense that patients get good care here. Even though it is crowded today, I am told that just several years ago, the hospital was overwhelmed with patients bearing bullet and shrapnel wounds from the civil war. When I close my eyes, the years melt away, and I can sense their presence and hear their cries. Stretchers and people, doctors and nurses, pleas for mercy, family members kneeling beside loved ones. Men, women, and children crowding the entrance with wounds, all needing attention. The smell of blood and fear everywhere. Although war may provide victory for some, it was in this hallway that the frightful price of the Sandinista revolution was paid. A hallway now swept clean and freshly painted—the grim drama wiped away, leaving no trace.

As in most developing countries, families stay with patients to attend their needs. There are mothers with each child in the pediatrics ward. And several family members chat with a new mother from behind a green curtain that divides the hallway from the OB ward. Despite ceilings that seem twenty feet high, the poor ventilation makes the corridor hot and sticky. I can hear the chatter of voices from several conversations echoing against the concrete walls. Someone is cooking lunch and the smell of fried chicken drifts past me.

I walk past the OB ward toward the operating suite. Curiously, a young woman sits alone, her face toward a white washed cement wall. Unlike most of the other patients, she has no visitors. No one has cooked for her; I hear no chatter from family or friends. I find it strange that she sits facing the wall—not facing the corridor. As I walk past, she turns. She is young, pretty. Her face deeply lined, her frame thin and pale. Her abundant, uncombed black hair tumbles onto her tattered, brown hospital gown. Her eyes seem tired, her countenance sad. She looks as if she is bearing some heavy burden, some torment crushing her, weighing her down. She glances toward me, but shows no expression, no acknowledgement of my presence. Without a suggestion of affirmation, she turns back to stare at the white wall.

As I walk past, her blank stare follows me. Later that day, thoughts of her sorrow still linger. Her eyes haunt me at night, like a ghostly apparition, when sleep escapes me. I have seen this too many times, in other hospitals, in other hallways, and in other countries. A young woman. A human shell. A living corpse. No purpose. No hope. No human comfort. Forgotten and unloved. So young yet believing all of life's possibilities have passed her by. So wrong. Because, if she only knew, still, at the end of broken dreams, He is the open door.[1]

---

[1] "People Need the Lord", Music by Phill McHugh and Greg Nelson, Words by Greg Nelson and Phill McHugh and Artist Steve Green

The Nurse

Her light, sandy-brown hair fell easily over her right shoulder as she knelt on the concrete in front of the old man. Her gloved hand, wet with sweat, was extended toward his black, callused foot. He leaned heavily on the ancient stick he used as a cane. His white hair was tousled, his face deeply lined from the years. The wound on his foot, covered with flies, was a deep red-purple with a yellow coating reminiscent of melted cheese. Her delicate fingers brushed aside the flies as she painstakingly and gently cleaned the wound. The aroma of her love filled the little clinic—the sweet fragrance of the knowledge of Christ. Several generations apart and from two vastly different worlds, sharing the same healing moment. Both consumed for the time in their own private thoughts, unaware of the more than two hundred Haitian onlookers who watched silently in astonishment.

I have watched those hands care for other wounds on other feet at other times and in other places. First as a student, then as a nurse. There had been the infected shotgun wound on the foot of a pastor in a remote area of the Amazon. And a tattered cast on a broken ankle high in the Andes. There had been imbedded thorns and open sores on the feet of children and flies that were brushed away from a foot that had been wrapped in a dirty cloth. The same light-brown hair, the same simple smile, the same tender touch. A bright-faced girl kneeling on concrete and mud at the feet of others. God's hands reaching down through hers. A letter written by the Spirit of God on a human heart. Grace, mercy, and healing dispensed with a smile, with sweat-drenched gloves and a bended knee. A gentle touch, a simple gesture—a girl, somehow now a woman. Love kneeling on concrete in a hot steamy jungle.

Thousands of years ago, another woman knelt to clean a man's feet. She washed them with her tears and dried them with her hair. She anointed them with a costly ointment, and the fragrance filled the room. A simple act indelibly burned into the collective consciousness of mankind for over two millennia. He, like the old Haitian man of today and the hundreds who watched, had been stunned by her offering. Love, kneeling down and not counting the cost. A declaration mightier than the edicts of governments. A force sufficiently strong to alter the course of history. A gift more precious than gold and healing lasting for eternity.

Photo by Ted Kuhn

Haitian Child

Belén Boatman

Belén

I quitos is a city of diversity. It has been the port of entry to the Peruvian Amazon for a hundred years and is an odd mixture of Spanish, Portuguese and tribal cultures. I spent my first night in Iquitos in an air-conditioned hotel. After my morning cup of Peruvian coffee, I walked the esplanade leading to the river. The comfortable row houses had been constructed of pastel colored tile imported from Portugal more than a century ago. The many wrought iron doors and windows had been imported from France on sailing ships and steamers that came several thousand miles up the Amazon along with the first American and British missionaries. On one corner stood a Peruvian military outpost with soldiers brandishing automatic weapons, guarding the high ground overlooking the river. On the opposite corner and underneath a sign advertising a modern day "Amazon Ecotour," workers poured concrete into the gaping holes of the pavement.

The esplanade provided a view of the great river and the warm breeze encouraged me on. Between my elevated walkway and the enormous river was a maze of slums that formed a half-mile wide buffer between the city and the great river. I descended a trash-strewn hill onto narrow board walkways that were the entrance into the expansive slums. A young man in a dugout canoe serving as a water taxi awaited my arrival at the river's edge.

With his mud-covered bare feet, he stepped on several small bronze-colored coins on the bow while he held the little dugout still for me. With one hand I gripped a bamboo pole and cautiously stepped from the suspended board where I was perched into the front of the dugout, trying not to fall. Once seated, the cocoa colored water was only an inch beneath the side of the canoe. There was no opportunity to readjust my weight. Even the smallest movement would flip the unstable canoe into the murky water. As we pushed off, paper and plastic bags floated in the muck along with unidentified organic matter. Children and adults peered down from elevated bamboo and thatched lofts that served as their homes. I felt as if I were trespassing, though not unwelcome. Just a gringo stranger in a dugout canoe slipping through the watery filth known as Belén.

A little girl passed us in her dugout. She smiled. An old man propped himself up with a stick on the front of another canoe, his deeply lined face expressionless. A woman with a pot of steamed rice and bananas, a floating restaurant, nearly ran her canoe into ours. It was mid-morning and people traveling the river would soon want lunch. A bamboo barge with bananas, coconuts and goats passed on their way from the Amazon River to the Belén market. An uninsulated electric wire coming from nowhere passed just over my head to a blaring radio in a broken down hut where a sign proclaimed "restaurant and disco". Obviously enjoying the sight, a little boy urinated in a fine arc from his elevated hut into the dirty brown water. Raw sewage from another hut fell a little too closely into the water beside me. A sign painted on the building identified the "Cholera Treatment Center" as we floated past.

My boatman circled back toward the shore, but as we approached, our little water taxi became stuck in the mud. I climbed onto a flimsy bamboo ladder and balancing once again on elevated, slippery, mud-covered mahogany boards, I picked my way toward dry land. We passed the area where the walkway had broken the week before sending a missionary named Rita neck deep into the sewage below. A little girl sat on one of the boards holding a hairless gray puppy with a large oozing sore on its head. I heard singing as I passed a one-room church where the boards ended and dry land began. Emaciated dogs slept soundly on the concrete steps leading from the riverfront up to the Belén open market. The air smelled of rotting vegetables and fish. Filth reminiscent of sticky brown sugar covered my open arms and face. Roving vendors hawked their wares, a cacophony of sounds. A garbage pile at the entrance of the market stood in front of the once attractive wrought iron pavilion brought from Europe a century before. The narrow walkways inside the market were bustling with activity. I watched in amazement as a young girl cleaned smoldering charcoal from a cooking grill with her bare hands, seemingly unconcerned about the burns. Salted and fresh fish were heaped in piles. Another table displayed a goat head with unseeing eyes staring into the crowded market. Sheep entrails hung from aloft. Yellow spices in a condom dangled from a bamboo pole. Exotic fruits ripened in the tropical sun. A man eating a raw fish leaned against a wall to rest, unaware of my presence as I passed by. A woman sat cross-legged behind a pile of fresh liver that oozed blood onto the table in front of her. An old man sat at a table rolling cut tobacco into cigarettes and binding them into packets. Thousands of people busy at their work.

Belén, Bethlehem in Spanish. Like the Bethlehem of years ago, a place of little or no account. Belén, a gigantic slum perched in the sewage of Iquitos. A place where the poor build elevated lofts over the watery muck—unable to purchase or rent land. Belén—poor, dirty, smelly. An insult to our senses. As objectionable to us as our sins must be to the heart of God.

Yet if Jesus were to be born today, would he not choose such a place as Belén? Would not street orphans gather around holding tightly to his garments, listening to his parables? Would he not tell us that of such is the kingdom of heaven? Would he not be a friend to the bar and disco owners, unworthy as they are, showing compassion on them? Belén, a slum fit for a king.

To the orphans and street children in a place known as Belén, to the disco owners, to the widows, to those who are hungry, to those stricken with cholera, to those dying without hope . . . "I have a message. He sees you. He knows you. He is with you. He loves you. Jesus loves you."[1]

"Whom shall I send and who will go for us?" [2] "For I was hungry and you gave me food . . . I was naked and you clothed me, I was sick and you visited me."[3] And the King will say, "As you did it to the least of these (in Belén) . . you did it to me."[4]

Until the day when He will wipe away every tear, and death shall be no more and there shall be no more mourning, crying or pain.[5] Until that day—"Here am I! Send me."[6]

---

[1] Excerpts from a song by Twila Paris
[2] Isaiah 6:8a RSV
[3] Matthew 25: 36–37 RSV
[4] Matthew 25: 40 RSV
[5] Revelation 21:4 RSV
[6] Isaiah 6: 8b RSV

Photo by Ted Kuhn

Belén

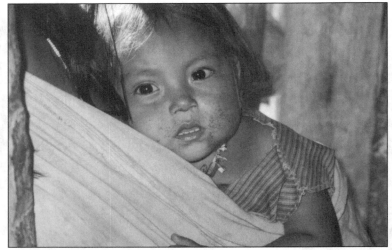

Photo by Lydia Kuhn

Nomatzieguenga Child with Monkey Tooth Necklace, Amazon Jungle

Little Baby Sleep

~~

Several weeks have passed since the devastating hurricane pillaged the coastal towns and mountain villages of Honduras. People are still struggling to bury their dead and piece together what is left of their broken lives. Roads are only now becoming passable. Our medical disaster team planned to meet in La Ceiba, having journeyed from different parts of the United States and Central America. We were to gather in the hotel restaurant for supper, giving us the evening to get acquainted and to physically and psychologically prepare for the next day's journey into the disaster zone.

Osbaldo and Amanda, our Cuban-American translators, had arrived at the restaurant ahead of the rest of the team. They decided to order while waiting for the team to assemble. By the time I arrived, they were finishing a plate of fried fish. I took a seat beside Osbaldo. The fish had been served whole, head and body attached with vegetables and rice on the side. Osbaldo had carefully separated the meat from the needle-like bones with his fork. He had neatly placed the bones, fin and part of the head on a small bone plate beside him.

From the corner of my eye, I caught a glimpse of three children peering through the open window of the restaurant from the street just inches from where I sat. They were dirty and barefoot, with no shirts and with sagging shorts tied around their tiny waists with frayed rope. Like street waifs from a Dickens story. They were remarkably courteous and well-behaved. I guessed they were brothers, or at least good friends, each leaning on the other, the oldest with his arm around the neck of the youngest. For a while, they just stood and stared through the window. Eventually, all three cautiously walked through the door of the restaurant, each holding on to the other for support. The oldest bent forward and spoke privately to Osbaldo. Osbaldo smiled, then nodded. The child scraped all the fish bones from the bone plate into his hand and ran out the door into the street and the darkness of the night.

After supper, I walked the streets of La Ceiba. This had once been a wealthy port city where bananas, pineapples, and tropical fruits had been shipped to the US on steamers docked at the pier near our hotel. The pier, now barely useable, was broken and in disrepair. Large chunks of concrete were missing and the blue Caribbean splashed through the gaping holes. Railroad ties that ran the length of the pier looked as if they had not been used in years. Twisted re-bar snaked from holes in every direction, making walking on the pier challenging if not downright dangerous. A tugboat was being loaded with food and supplies for one of the outer islands devastated by the hurricane. The tug seemed to be sitting perilously low in the water under the weight of her cargo.

Moored next to the tug was a sleek luxury yacht. Multiple antennas and a satellite dish protruded from her bridge like tentacles. The yacht was quite a contrast to the tug—new and clean with deck hands in matching uniforms and sailor caps. A British flag on the bow. Two middle-aged men, dressed in white with broad hats were sitting in lounge chairs sipping whiskey from a glass. They turned their chairs away from the pier and laughed at some private joke. Not more than fifteen feet from the yacht, several men fished from a hole in the pier using small, unbaited hooks trying to snare fingerlings for their supper. The once white, sandy beach was strewn with litter. And where American and European vacationers had once sunned themselves, a shantytown now stood constructed of cardboard and tin. Liquid sewage trickled from the shacks across the beach and into the Caribbean.

I turned from the pier to walk back to the hotel. The glow of the evening was past and night had fallen across the beaches—the moon only a sliver in the darkness. A man clad in torn underwear rummaged in a trash can along the street. A sign for an American Ecotour company proclaimed, "Temporarily closed due to hurricane." Three American soldiers dressed in fatigues huddled over an ATM machine in the front of a bank lobby. As I stared at the three American soldiers, I nearly stepped on the hand of an infant asleep on the sidewalk—the baby lying beside his sleeping mother. The child's partially clenched fist outstretched. Both slept, apparently unaware and unconcerned about the unsure footing of strangers.

I have seen hungry people many times and I have stepped over multitudes of sleeping children in the slums of cities around the world. I have seen the naked rummage through trash and women scavenge refuse looking for a morsel to eat. And I have watched the wealthy turn their backs on the poor to engage in endless chatter. But, I didn't expect this, not here, not so close to home. Those are other places—places hard to get to and far away.

The vision of the baby sleeping on the sidewalk disturbs my sleep. I am restless knowing that the child is sleeping on the street only a few yards from my hotel room. Perhaps I should go, search for them and bring them into the safety of the hotel room. Yet, I do not go. Cars race up and down the street outside my window. Each time I awaken, I imagine the little hand on the dirty pavement. People pass by, seeing but not seeing, pretending not to notice, not to care. Finally sleep comes and I dream. I dream that I step on the baby's hand. The clenched fist opens, exposing several neatly cleaned fish bones.

Photo by Lydia Kuhn

Child, Slums of Nairobi

Noella

Our medical team had been working in the villages hardest hit by hurricane Mitch—providing dawn-to-dusk medical care in churches and homes hit with massive devastation and untold suffering. Each morning, hundreds lined up to be treated. Local pastors and deacons struggled to maintain some degree of order. It was hard to turn away people who were sick and had lost everything. That is where I first met Noella—a 16-year-old from the Aguan Valley of Honduras, from the village of Coyelles Reyes. She was attractive in spite of weighing only sixty pounds, with a sweet smile and an easy, comfortable disposition. The kind of girl you could fall in love with at first sight. When I met her, she had long, silky, black hair carefully and neatly combed, framing her tan face and held in place by a small brochette. She wore a clean and neatly pressed white blouse, which was much too large for her thin frame but provided a striking contrast to her long, tumbling black hair.

Noella, a beautiful young woman but dying slowly of some unknown disease. When I listened to her lungs with my stethoscope, she pulled her blouse over her breasts—self-conscious and embarrassed by her thin, wasted body. Desperately sick, but still able to maintain her dignity. Two months earlier she had been able to walk. Now, too weak to lift herself from bed.

In the midst of thousands of needy people, there was something about Noella that stirred our emotions. Maybe it was that she was a pretty young woman. Maybe it was that pretty young women should not die. Or maybe it was God working in us—or perhaps a combination. No, we could not save every one who was sick or injured in post-hurricane Honduras, but just maybe we could save one. The church met and was divided. Helping her meant not helping others, equally needy. Using our time and resources for Noella, meant others, names and faces unknown to us, might die. Even her family could not agree. Our conversation went long into the night. Noella overheard. I watched her as she wept quietly.

Several of us carried Noella to the truck and lay her across the back seat of the cab. The 45-minute trip to Olanchito exhausted her. The hospital at first unsure they would accept her; after all, she was from a poor family, and bills would have to be paid. Her problem was in her brain. She would most likely die, and would not the resources be better spent elsewhere? She would need a CT scan and neurologist, available only in Tegucigalpa. She lay on the hard gurney for several hours while her future was debated, never complaining. Maybe it is a tumor, maybe an abscess, we argued. Maybe curable, maybe not. Shouldn't a pretty 16-year-old with long black hair and a sweet disposition be given a chance?

I returned to the United States not knowing her fate. Months later, I heard that Noella had made the trip to Tegucigalpa and was admitted to a hospital. The church arranged for her travel and several church members accompanied her. They must have decided that her life was indeed precious, precious in the sight of God.

I never learned what became of her. Her story, like those of many of the Christians in post-hurricane Honduras, is unknown. Perhaps a wonderful story of healing and restoration; perhaps a story of suffering and death. Yet one thing is known, the church gathered together, and bore the burden of her illness, providing comfort, fellowship, and love for the dying Noella. The church of Christ, faithful in the end.

Sometimes I wonder if the church is a body, whether the believers in Honduras might be the toes. They are small appendages rarely noticed, entrusted with no seeming great task. Encrusted with dirt, walking barefoot in the mud. Poor and most often forgotten. Dying without anyone noticing. But it is the toes that touch the earth first. When the toes are broken, the body cannot go forward. When the toes are cut off, the body is unstable and falls. The entire Body of Christ, standing on the faith of the Christians in Honduras?

Yet I have a dream. I have a dream that one day I will return to the Aguan Valley—to the little village of Coyelles Reyes, and a pretty young woman will meet me there. A pretty young woman named Noella. And her long, silky hair will gently fall over her white blouse, held back only by a small brochette, framing her tan face and sweet smile.

Photo by Ted Kuhn

Chin Hills, Myanmar

The Cup of Tea

The rice had been harvested for months and the flat brown paddies now stood dormant. Beautiful golden fields stretched for miles, dotted by an occasional royal palm. I was back in Asia. A strange and exotic place, yet I felt oddly at home. Cows and water buffalo crossed in front of our old truck as we swerved to avoid potholes and people. This once wealthy nation had exported rice, tea, and teak to many of her Asian neighbors. Her tea had filled the cups of the world for generations, and the wood on the decks of ships for a century had come from her forests. The glory of the past had faded, nearly forgotten, a nation reduced to poverty under socialist dictatorships. Pockets that had once bulged with prosperity were replaced by torn and tattered clothing. This part of Asia had been without missionaries for decades. Nevertheless, the church had grown. Life had sometimes been brutal for these warm and generous people who bore their persecution like a coat quickly removed. I dared to imagine that God would have a special place in His crown for precious jewels such as these.

We left the main road and drove a short distance on a dusty lane. Women squatting around a basin washing clothes paused to observe as we passed. Vehicles were still regarded as somewhat novel in this village area. A pastor had started a new church and had moved here to be near his congregation. As we approached, his house seemed small, simple but well appointed. Several of his children greeted us with cries of excitement. His wife, barely showing in the middle of her pregnancy, welcomed us with a gracious smile. Sensing unspoken trust, I picked up her smallest child and carried him on my shoulder into the house. No pretenses here and nothing to hide. Pleasant, honest, hospitable, and genuinely delighted to welcome us.

The inside of the house was as simple as the outside. The only decoration was a calendar from 1994 showing a glossy print of several farmers in a rice paddy. Taped to a cupboard was an ancient black and white photo, even those colors faded with age. A family portrait, I guessed. Someone's grandparents or great-grandparents at a celebration long since passed. Yet for at least one person in this home, it symbolized a distant memory, important yet fading with the passing years. Children of differing ages played on the floor, delighted to be back at their games now that the visitors had been welcomed. A four-year-old jumped up and down and growled at his younger brother, pretending to be a tiger. His brother, on cue, screamed with feigned fright and ran to hide behind his mother's dress. His brother the tiger ran circles around him, growling until they both collapsed in gleeful exhaustion. Their father, the pastor, was visiting one of the members; he should return shortly.

Shall we take some tea, my friend asked? Of course, I responded. A few moments later I heard the pastor's wife putting water into a kettle. An aluminum pot rested on a small open fire and within minutes, steam poured from its spout.

She brought my tea first. Bowing almost imperceptibly, and without a smile, she presented the cup almost like an offering. The cup and saucer were made of fine bone china. Even though these were well-educated people, I considered china would be very unusual in a poor village area. The cup was delicate and light, like the special china cups my grandmother used for Thanksgiving so many years ago. My father and uncle would sit around the table and drink coffee from cups like these, smoking cigars and speaking of football and investments. They were the kind with umber-colored designs etched into the china and finger holes not quite large enough. Yet, these cups were old. Very old. I could easily envision British businessmen sipping tea from these very china cups discussing the affairs of the empire at some far pavilion a half century or more ago. The saucer was perfect, but the cup had its stem broken. There were several chips on the rim and a miniscule crack ran about half way down the teacup. She presented a similar cup to my friend. I glanced into the cup. Just boiling water—no sign of tea. My friend did the same. Our eyes met, but neither spoke. "Thank you," I responded. Would I take sugar in my tea, she asked. She presented a matching bowl with a few granules of coarse brown sugar strewn across the bottom. Looking first into the bowl and then at the children playing at my feet, I responded, "No, I'll have my tea just like this."

She sat with us, no cup for her. We smiled and sipped hot water. We talked about things people talk about while sipping tea. We spoke about the weather, our families and upcoming events, the arrival of the new baby. And we asked each other about our children. We mentioned a woman in the church and her poor health. How we should remember to pray for her. We all agreed that we needed to visit more often. Conversation exhausted, hot water consumed, she removed our teacups. Marvelous hospitality we agreed. We begged her permission to leave, said a short prayer and hugged each child in turn.

Driving back, neither of us spoke. We have not spoken of it since. A mutual conspiracy of silence. A shared agony of the spirit. Our brother and sister. And a cup of hot water.

Since that afternoon, I suppose, I have had many cups of tea and coffee. Coffee for breakfast and cappuccino in American airports. I have delighted in the milky sweet chai of the African high plains. I have savored the aroma of a rich dark coffee in Honduras, and café con leche in Lima. Yet, now and then, when I stare out of the cafés, the coffee shops, the airport kiosks, or just into the quiet of the night, I think back to a very special cup of tea.

With children playing at my feet, tea served in the finest bone china. An ancient teacup with its own legacy and a broken stem. Presented as an offering. A shared conspiracy of silence. And to this day, no one knows the closely guarded secret, joy and sorrow mixed together, in that special cup of tea.

Archona

We lived in a simple two-room house just south of
Faridpur town. A local teacher had previously lived
there, but it had been vacant for years when we moved
in. A good cleaning and some white wash on the walls, and it became home. Although we had no running water and electricity
only occasionally, we did have an outside squat toilet and a tin
roof. Thus we lived in relative luxury by Bengali standards. Behind
the toilet was a row of banana trees that led a short distance to the
railroad tracks. In the early morning, just at dawn, an ancient steam
engine ran north to Rajbari, returning to Faridpur again before
sunset in the late afternoon.

We had neighbors outside our bedroom window. A poor Hindu
family made a makeshift house with walls of jute and a roof of
thatch in front of our banana trees. Squatter's rights. No one seemed
to care. In fact, no one seemed to notice. An invisible family. We
could lie in bed and look through the open bars of our window
into their thatched home. Privacy was never an issue. In the early
morning, the children would peek through the bars of our window to see if we were awake. "Memshib, memshib, are you still
sleeping?" We greeted each new day the same way. Smiling faces

peering into our bedroom, hands outstretched to touch our hair through the mosquito netting over our plank bed.

Our "neighbors" had several children, all girls. Most were their own, but others came from who-knows-where. Perhaps from distant relatives who could not afford to feed their children? They sent them from the village to the relative prosperity of the city. When they came to greet us in the morning, they all came. The older girls carried the smaller ones and infants on their hips. It was a pleasant time of day. The time between awakening when the haze was still clearing from the jungle and the smoke of cooking fires first began to fill the air, until the time when household chores would begin and Sharon and I would leave for the clinic. It was a routine that filled our early mornings for the years we lived in Faridpur. A routine that we looked forward to and a routine that we enjoyed.

There was an older girl of ten or twelve who always stood toward the back and never spoke. She wore the same dirty dress every day, a little smock that had made the long journey from the West courtesy of some relief organization. She carried a scrawny child on her hip. This child was not the daughter of our neighbors but had come to their household from somewhere else. She apparently could not walk or stand and thus had to be carried. We could easily see the telltale muscle-wasting of her legs. Her thin face and bloated belly told the rest of the story. Because she was not their daughter, and because she was a girl and sick, they gave her little food. Why waste perfectly good food on a little girl that won't survive anyway, we were told? That is how we came to know and love Archona.

One day we invited Archona to breakfast. She stayed a year and a half. I remember her on that first day struggling to sit upright in our kitchen. Skinny legs askew providing no support. We gave her a boiled egg and some milk. She mashed the egg on the floor with her fingers and ate only a small portion of the hard yolk. Later she had diarrhea on the kitchen floor and refused to drink the milk. No. We would have to begin more slowly. Yet day by day, with food, love and attention, Archona became stronger.

In a month or two, she stood and took several wobbly steps. By three months she was walking, and in six months she could awkwardly run. We began to take her to church and her "sisters" would tag along. After a year we arranged for her to go to school. We watched her like proud parents each morning in her clean clothes, carrying her notebook, walking to school with the other children. Her legs still skinny but her bloated belly now gone. Black, shiny hair neatly washed and combed. A pretty little gift from God, on loan for just a time.

Another year passed and our work took us further into the rural areas. It became impractical for us to travel each day. We decided to move into a new house deep in the village. Archona, now healthy, would be returned to the care of her "parents," our next door neighbors. We provided money for the next year of school and a little extra for food. We would visit when we could. We only saw her several times that first year. I last visited her many years later when she was eleven. I saw her running along the railroad tracks. A pretty little wisp of a girl who hugged me and called me "dada"—older brother. She dropped out of school, sufficiently strong to work.

Now, sometimes when I sit in front of my television in Augusta, I startle and imagine I see her. A little girl on the hip of an older child. Skinny dangling arms and legs. A bloated belly and an expression of hopelessness. Year after year the names of the places change, Bangladesh is no longer in the news. Bosnia, Rwanda, Somalia. The children all seem the same. No, I cannot save all the children of the world. But I can save a few. Archona, wherever you are, I still love you.

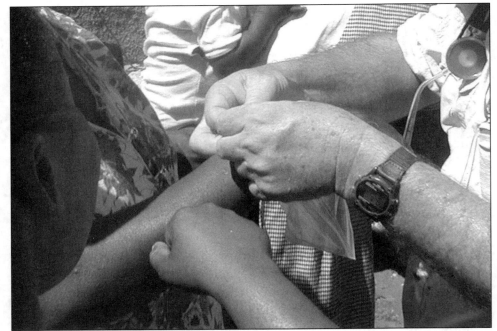

Ted Giving Gospel Bracelets in Haiti

The String of Beads

I would like to tell you the story of how my life was saved." She held up a small black thread with five colored beads for everyone to see. The morning sun was hot. Sweat dripped down my neck and back as I stood on a mud path between houses in the village of St. Marc. "These beads tell the story," she said. The crowd shuffled. A baby cried. Several more curious onlookers joined the already substantial crowd. All eyes locked on a diminutive, fair skinned, blonde woman. I held the heavy megaphone amplifier at my waist, she spoke into the mike. Charles stood beside me to translate. It seemed all so . . . strange, yet all so familiar. I, an academic physician turned street evangelist in a hot, dusty village on the northern shore of Haiti. If anyone was a fool for Christ, I thought, it had to be me, and it had to be now.

"The gold bead represents heaven," she continued. There was a momentary pause as Charles translated into Creole. "God has prepared a wonderful place for you. No more crying, no pain, no suffering, no death and no sickness. Would you like to go there?" A few heads nodded. Others now came to join the crowd pushing in from the back. A sea of black faces-covered with sweat. Several children playing with sticks in the mud by my feet stopped their play to listen.

"The black bead represents things we do that make God sad. Things He told us not to do, but we do anyway. It is the blackness of our hearts. We cannot be together with Him when we do these awful things. These things separate us from His love." Now the crowed murmured, openly sharing some secret. It was a while before we could regain control. They were all listening. Even the children. I could tell they knew about sin. Gradually eyes refocused on the string of beads. "What can we do?" she asked. A slow Creole chorus of "What can we do? What can we do?" rippled through the crowd.

I had watched the same confusion spread over crowds in other cities and other countries. In a Haitian village the day before I had watched the same drama. In Manila, my eyes had locked on a man with leprosy in a street center for the homeless. I watched as he had pondered the same question. His eyes spoke the words that his lips were forbidden to pronounce. "What can I do?" A man at the back of today's crowd raised his hand and pointed a bony finger toward the sky. I suspected he was pointing toward God. As my eyes traced the movement of his hand, I saw the red flag of a voodoo temple directly behind him. I had not noticed it before. I was standing at the very threshold of the synagogue of Satan.

"The red bead is the blood of Jesus—God's son. God sacrificed His son for us so that our sins could be forgiven. Jesus paid for our sins so that you and I can be together with God." "Oh," the crowd exhaled. Heads nodded in approval. An answer, an open door—a perceived way out of the dilemma. An old man sitting in a chair toward the back put his head on his lap and wept openly.

I had witnessed this anguish in the villages of Montrious and Messailler. And in the Philippines in Lipa City, and Val's church near the garbage mountain. The expression as men and women finally understood the purpose of the blood. A sudden revelation—comprehension and remorse over sin. The Spirit of God working in human hearts. The sin, the blood, the sacrifice, the reconciliation. The awful necessity of it all.

"The white bead is how we appear to God when Jesus' blood cleans us as white as snow." I nervously laughed. No one in any of these villages had ever seen snow. "White linen," she corrected, "just washed and bleached." Heads nodded.

"The last bead is the green bead. It represents growth because God wants us to know about Him—just like you want to know all about someone you love. He wants us to know about Him and to grow to love Him and to be like Him." "Oui," pronounced a chorus in unison. "You can read His story in the Bible." She held a copy of a Bible in her other hand beside the string of beads.

"Who wants to pray to receive this free gift that God has given us in Jesus?" she said. "Raise your hands". A throng of black hands waved in the morning sunlight. My mind again flashed to the man with leprosy in the homeless shelter in Manila, bursting with joy—so anxious and excited to give his life to Christ. He had raised both hands high in the air and waved them back and forth. Hands with no fingers lifted as a precious gift to God.

"Lord, I know that I have done things that hurt you." A pause, the translation in Creole then the murmur of a hundred voices. Heads bowed. Eyes closed. "Lord, forgive me," she said. Again a pause, a translation and again a hundred voices in solemn prayer. A woman wept softly, unable to hold the tide of emotion. A baby cried and was quickly put on its mother's breast. "Wash me with Jesus' blood, so I might be clean inside like bleached linen." Another petition, another pause, another translation and another prayer. "Help me to love you so that we can be together. Amen."

"I would like to give you one of these bracelets if you prayed with me," my companion said, holding high the bracelet. A hundred people crowded toward us. My vision blocked by a sea of black wrists. I grabbed the first wrist. "God bless you," I said embracing a young woman. Then the smell of dust and sweat. Hands grabbing my hand. A tug on my shirt. A woman thrusting her baby forward. Wide smiles, white teeth, black faces. The old, the young. Suddenly it stopped. It was complete. I stood trembling, shaken by the power of the moment. An elderly Haitian woman had been watching me from a distance. She stepped over a mud puddle, blue bandana covering white hair. Embracing me, she kissed me on the cheek. I wept. She held me.

I have witnessed this simple message on other hot mornings in other crowded places. Multitudes pushing and desperate to hear. Dark eyes riveted on a string of beads. A simple prayer whispered but heard in highest heaven. Hearts broken, then restored. A sea of wrists. Black, brown, yellow. Indian, Hispanic, Asian. Many times I have stood trembling under the awesome power of God's grace. But today, sitting here in my home a thousand miles from that dusty street in St. Marc, it seems almost foolish. Yet so simple. So profound. So powerful. So wonderful. So right. And so free.

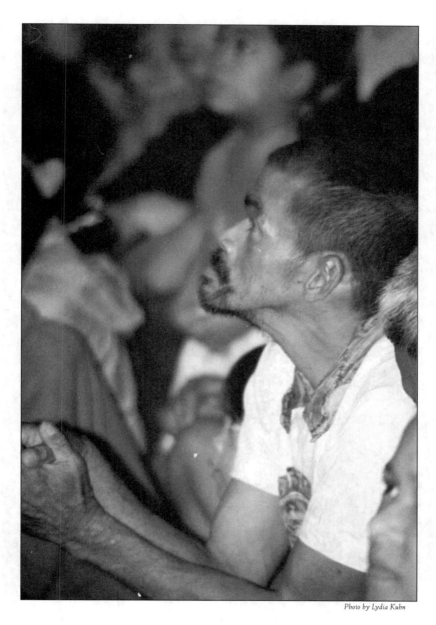

Photo by Lydia Kuhn

Man with Leprosy Accepting Christ
in Slums of Manila

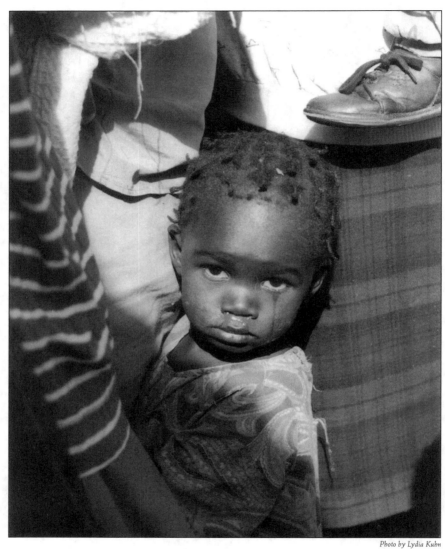

Photo by Lydia Kuhn

Slums of Nairobi

Was It Worthwhile?

I t is my first day back to work after returning from Honduras. I
am exhausted from the long hours of patient care in the wake
of the devastation wrought by hurricane Mitch. Although the
emergency department is full of patients, my heart and mind are
full of questions and a part of me is still in Central America. Was it
worthwhile? Did the medical team make a difference? Would the
people of the Aguan Valley have been better off if we had just sent
them the money spent on airfare and support?

I remember the parable of pulling drowning people out of a
river. It is often used as an argument against curative medical
services. It goes something like this: I can work all day and night
until I am exhausted pulling drowning people out of the river,
but it is only when I discover why they are falling in upstream,
and prevent them from falling in, that I can really make a difference. I have spent the last several weeks pulling drowning people
out of a river, and I am certainly exhausted. I even knew why they
were falling in upstream and I knew how to prevent them from
falling. Nevertheless, I spent these weeks as a lifeguard and constructed no fence upstream. How can I justify my actions to others and defend the expense and resources spent on curative
medicine in rural Honduras?

An emergency medicine resident asks me to see a patient. He presents a middle-aged woman with advanced breast cancer. She has a metastatic lesion in her back causing her constant, severe pain. She is unable to lie down or stand comfortably and recently developed weakness in her legs—the tumor expanding to her spinal cord. A "slam-dunk" for the resident—an easy patient. Order an MRI and admit to neurosurgery for decompression. Yet, speaking with her breaks my heart. She is frail and covers her head with a bandana, having lost her hair from chemotherapy. She grimaces in pain as we talk. She looks older than her years and much older than her husband—weeks of pain and suffering having taken their toll. She asks for pain relief and I give her morphine. For the moment she rests, her pain relieved. I know that soon the pain will return. We both know that in the next several days the cancer will claim her frail life. Her short future will be filled with days of discomfort as she struggles with the pain and good-byes to family and friends. I left the room but returned to check on her. She stirred and held out her hand. I extended mine. And for a moment our hands and lives touched. She wanted to thank me for the care I provided, then closed her eyes and fell back to sleep. I had thought of asking if the morphine helped, but I already knew the answer.

Ask a drowning man if he desires rescue. Ask him, even if he knows he will fall in again. What is the value of another day? Another week? A month? A year? What would his answer be? What would your answer be? Is temporary relief of pain or healing worthwhile? Indeed, it is priceless! Mercy extended in love. Even in this age of high-speed technology, physical and spiritual healing nevertheless proceed at the pace of one life touching another. Is temporary relief of suffering worthwhile? Look into the eyes of the woman dying of breast cancer. Or look into the eyes of a Honduran mother who has lost everything. And you will know the answer.

Remember Me[†]

~~

Her leathery brown face tilted awkwardly back, her jaw hung loosely open. Eyes covered with a dry, white haze stared blindly at the ceiling. Open, but unseeing. Unkempt thin white hair lay wildly against the pillow. Wasted arms and legs rested neatly on the stretcher. An inoperable brain tumor with a GI bleed. An NG tube taped to her nose drained black, granular material. "Will she make it to the floor?" I asked. "I'm not sure, but she is a DNR," he said. "If she codes, just let her go."

An hour passed before I returned to resuscitation room 8. She lay in exactly the same position. NG taped to her nose, head pitched back, glazed over eyes fixed on the tiles of the ceiling, staring into eternity. There was a softly heard groan, like a long, slow, sigh coming from her lips. Shaking, faltering, but clearly discernable. I remembered hearing it before when I was in the room. Turning to her son and daughter at the foot of the stretcher, I asked, "Does she always make this noise?"

"She is singing", her daughter said, eyes filling with tears. I listened more intently, leaning my ear over the gaping mouth. The soft groan did indeed have a musical quality. "What is she singing?"

"Her favorite hymn, 'Remember Me.'"

Another hour passed. The admitting team had been held up with another patient. She laid in the same position, unmoving, seemingly unaware of her surroundings, unseeing eyes staring into the future. Still the music continued. "I have never heard of this hymn."

"Then we will sing it together for you." As the words of an old Negro Spiritual, full of sorrow, passion and hope came from their lips, a profound hush fell upon my spirit.

> O Lord, I'm your child
> O Lord, I'm your child
> O Lord, I'm your child
> O Lord, Remember me!

Another hour passed. Resuscitation room 8 had been cleaned and awaited the arrival of another patient. There was no trace of its former occupant. No trace of the impact on the clean, bright room from the eternal drama of an hour ago.

"Miss Viola, did He remember you?"

†Previously published by Hanley & Belfus: *Remember Me, Annals of Emergency Medicine*, Volume 36, No 4, October 2000, pages 396–7. Used by permission.

Trauma Room 1[†]

Her feet were slightly dirty, resting on their heels, legs apart, and toes pointed outward from the bottom of the stretcher. Her young, naked body only a slightly different hue from the white sheet she lay upon. Breasts never meant to be exposed to the harsh lights of the trauma room, exposed for anyone to see. Her long, yellow hair bloodstained red. A small hole with powder burns just above the right ear, execution style. A grief stricken respiratory therapist anxiously squeezed the bag. Alarms sounded and console lights blinked off their warnings. A man in blue said, "Homicide-suicide." Someone whispered in my ear, "I have a fifteen-year-old daughter". "So do I," I remember answering. Two men in scrubs casually discussed how the police were having trouble identifying the shooter, his face blown off and cold on the sidewalk. Perfect justice, they agreed.

A small crowd gathered as usual outside the room, morbidly observing the drama. Eyes and conversation directed toward the naked body of a sixteen-year-old with long blonde hair. Others passed by, quickly looking the other way, avoiding emotional involvement and blocking bothersome images. In a few hours, in the quiet of the night, phones would ring in several homes throughout the country—an early Christmas for a select few. A heart has been found, a kidney that matches yours. A gift from the dead to the dying.

With the drama over, the paperwork done, the room cleaned and no trace left of the indescribable tragedy, I left the ER through the ambulance entrance. A short walk, a short drive, then to bed for the night. A group of high school students gathered just outside the ambulance bay. A tall, thin, slightly built girl was weeping on the shoulders of a young man. Long blonde hair to her waist, a halter top and jeans. By all measures a beauty, nearly the twin of the recent occupant of Trauma Room 1. If the dead could speak, what would she say? So physically mature, and yet so emotionally unprepared. Whatever happened to our children?

---

†Previously published as: "Trauma Room 1" *Academic Emergency Medicine*, Vol 7, No 7, July 2000, page 823. Used by permission.

Damaris

⁓

S he lives only a few steps from the main path that winds through the slum of Ongata Rongi. I had walked the path several times and never noticed her home before. We were making visits to AIDS patients who were too frail to travel the short distance to the church. Her house was made of native stone with a slanted tin roof and sagging, rotting, weathered, wooden beams. The door was quite small, only large enough for a child or small woman. My pack brushed against the top of the doorframe as I stooped to pass through. The inside was unexpectedly dark—a cheerless contrast to the bright sunshine outside. The front room was filled with smoke from an open cooking fire. The caustic fumes burned my eyes, and it amazed me how anyone could live in such a small, smoke-filled, unventilated room. An opening only half the size of the front door led to an adjoining room. I pushed my body through and entered a black, crypt-like space. I could sense the presence of another person, but my eyes, not accustomed to the dark, gave me few clues.

I switched on my flashlight. There was a wooden cot pushed to one side of the room. My knees barely touched the cot while my back pressed against the opposite wall. I felt like I had inadvertently wandered into a small cave. Clothes were hanging from the wooden rafters. The floor was dirt and the stones were cold. There was a damp, musty smell, and the odor of cold sweat permeating air that had not circulated for days.

There was an orange blanket draped over the empty cot, yet the blanket almost imperceptibly moved. Two brown, hollow eyes stared from beneath the blanket, transfixed by the beam of light like a deer suddenly frozen in headlights. Sunken cheeks, a nearly hairless head and the bony skeleton of what appeared to have been a young woman. Legs and arms, wasted and too weak to support weight, a living portrait of death camps from times gone by. There were urine stains on the sheet. Her lips moved yet made no sound. I had met Damaris.

I opened the small shutter a crack to let in the morning sunlight. She squinted, the light painful to her dark-accustomed eyes. Her wasted body even more grotesque in the soft sunlight. She was a woman of thirty-two. Staring into her face, I wondered, in a strange way, whether at one time she might have been pretty. Someone's lover or wife. And not as bold as I imagined the biblical Damaris, who had enthusiastically responded to Paul's public invitation in Athens. This African Damaris had a weakened, disease-ravaged body leaving her unable to stand. Her room served as a self-imposed prison cell. Yet like the biblical Damaris, one of God's precious daughters. Dying by degrees, alone in claustrophobic darkness, life going on just outside her closed window. We gave her medicine to help her swallow. She swished the white liquid in her mouth then vomited the milky substance on my friend's pant leg. I doubted she would do any better with the multivitamins.

There were several children ranging in ages from four to twelve. They had been outside playing when I first entered. "Who will care for her children?" I asked. "We haven't discussed it," my colleague replied. Damaris, just another unfolding tragedy among countless millions, in countless homes, in countless villages dying of AIDS in sub-Saharan Africa. In a few days or perhaps a week or two, the children playing outside will be orphans. Left alone without a mother, without food, without a home and, barring the benevolence of some organization, without hope for a better future. I had come here to meet her and her children for both the first and last time. We prayed, kneeling on the moist, dirt floor. As we prayed, she mouthed inaudible words, cracked, bleeding lips making no detectable sound. A prayer heard only by God. "We will visit if we can," we assured her. Then we walked out of her life forever, leaving the tragedy behind us like a discarded newspaper bearing yesterday's news.

AIDS attacks men and women by the very means God intended for blessing—His precious gift of relationship—a time when men and women are privileged to participate with the creator of all life, in the creation of new life. And that life in His own image. A curse instead of blessing. Separation instead of intimacy. Suffering instead of fellowship. Death instead of new birth. AIDS, an abomination to the gospel. And the sins of the parents are visited upon the children. A generation of children, innumerable millions, destined to die, robbed of the abundance of life by the ones who should have cherished them most. And those too numerous to count, often seem to count for nothing.

The future of Damaris, her children, and indeed the future of Africa is in the blood. Blood can bear life or death, blessing or curse. There is the giving of blood that saves and sustains, and defiled blood that bears death and sorrow. Sin that is covered by blood and sin that is brought on by blood. There is the blood of the covenant, and there is the blood that cries out. There is the sprinkled blood that speaks more graciously than the blood of Abel. Blood that cleanses us from guilt. And blood guiltiness. There is blood that brings us into fellowship with God and blood that separates us from the love of God. Atonement through blood. Condemnation through blood. Blood sufficient for all, or blood not sufficient at all. Sins that only the blood of the Lamb can atone and sins that the blood of lambs could never atone.

Yet, I will always remember the day I met you. There, in a far away land, in a little stone hut, along a dusty path, that leads through a slum called Ongata Rongi. Abandoned and dying of AIDS. You, alone in a small, dark room—the summation of the legacy of our generation. The biblical namesake of a woman from

Athens, known to the Apostle Paul. A woman of character and strength. A woman of faith. Damaris. Did angels bend near to listen as you prayed, your parched lips moving but making no sound? Did the Body of Christ comfort you in your time of need? And your children? And what could possibly be our testimony, when we were silent for so long? When we knew, but did not respond. When we were able, yet unwilling. Unengaged, mute witnesses to enormous tragedy? Proclaiming Christ's love, when mercy was far from us.

Ted with Children in Ongata Rongi, A Slum of Nairobi

Children in Slum of Nairobi

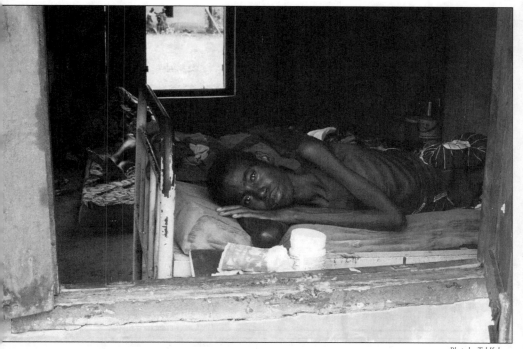

Woman Dying in Sub-Saharan Africa

Photo by Lydia Kuh

The Face of Sub-Saharan Africa

Farewell to the Last Spring

⁓

D roplets of fresh dew glisten on the delicate yellow rose cling-
ing to the white trellis in the morning sun. It's spring in
Georgia and the air is full of beauty, hope, and new life.
The view from my front porch is fresh, colorful, and reviving. Confederate jasmine budding, yet still lacking a few days before releas-
ing its intoxicating fragrance. A mud wasp flies motionless,
suspended in time, approaching a crack in a broken shutter. Squir-
rels scurry, gathering acorns. A bird crafts a nest in the fork of an
ancient water oak, Spanish moss draped majestically over the limb.
The sun on my face is warm and inviting. I am at home, at rest, at
peace, and loved.

It is hard to remember that only a few days ago, I walked the
colorless hallways of Manila's infectious disease hospital. It now
seems more like a thousand years. The malaria ward had been
nearly empty due to the dry season. I noted resting mosquitoes
on the walls of the dengue ward, perhaps digesting their latest
blood meal. A young woman with the dengue rash lay in bed
eating supper with her husband and children. I had purposely
walked slowly past the rabies ward. There were black steel bars
across the door. Patients locked in, a potential threat to the staff.
The newly dead body of an eleven-year-old boy lay shrouded

inside. Steel bars flung open—the child no longer a threat, just a pediatric casualty in a microscopic war. More wards, more patients, more hallways. Nurses doing chores. Residents writing on charts. The smell of disinfectant. Chipped paint. Private conversations in hushed tones. Overhanging white signs here and there: meningitis, chicken pox, dengue, measles and cholera.

The tuberculosis ward was isolated from the main hospital. A low, one-story structure of nondescript construction. Benches with idle patients lined the hallways. There was a musty smell. Deadly bacilli, too small for the human eye to see, filled the air. My physician friend had pulled a handkerchief from his pocket and covered his mouth and nose. Instinctively I held my breath. Past the first ward, then around the corner to the next. Unable to hold my breath any longer I decided to take short shallow breaths in a vain attempt to limit my own exposure.

Halfway down the next corridor we came upon the tuberculosis dying room. A large rectangular room, it had windows for viewing from the hallway. It was the designated place for patients with overwhelming infection or drug resistance. Fourteen beds. No nurses or residents running in or out. Isolated, alone. Unlike other patients on other wards, they did not turn to look or stare. No smiles, no greeting. Patients unwilling to be even momentarily distracted from the grave business of the day. Two beds held newly shrouded bodies. Sentinels, neatly wrapped in white, waiting patiently for someone, perhaps anyone, who cared. The barely living and the newly dead, side by side. Emaciated bodies, hollow cheeks, blank stares. Despair written in their eyes. Expressions of silent acceptance and hopelessness. Separated by us, for us. The living dead nearing the end of their last journey. One door in, one way out.

I am alone on my front porch in the warm Georgia sun enjoying life's simple pleasures. Content to be here—yet an inconvenient memory hangs over me. My cup of coffee empty, the tasks of the day beckon like an unsolicited intrusion into the quiet. The mud wasp is now safely hidden inside the shutter. A honeybee visits the yellow rose. My daughter readies for school. Cars to be driven, meetings to make, and events of the day that will suppress the painful vision of the dying room and the questions I am afraid to ask, and even if asked, dare not attempt to answer. Why me? Why the good fortune of birth and God's special grace? What special merit has placed me on my springtime Georgia porch and not on the stretchers of the dying room? In the counsel of the Almighty before the foundations of the earth, why was I chosen? And the knowledge that to whom much is given, much is expected.

The beauty of springtime in Georgia; a lifeless rectangular room in Manila. The fragrance of confederate jasmine; the musty smell of antiseptic. A yellow rose; the gray corridors. The green leaves; the white shrouds waiting for someone, anyone. Anticipation for tomorrow; despair sufficient for today. New life, and no life. Many roads to take, only one way out. The task of living, the task of dying. And the bittersweet sorrow of a farewell to the last spring.

Photo by Lydia Kuhn

Nomatzieguenga Mother and Child, Amazon Jungle

The Mystery of God's Love

I returned from the Amazon one week ago. It is hard to comprehend the amazing journey I completed. The tribal people of the Amazon seem so distant now, so remote. Even my thoughts and memories about them are fading. I flip through the photographs, and I can still remember. Yet, I do not sense the enormity of the jungle. I cannot smell the cooking fires, and the heat of the day is gone. I do not brush away the flies. The simple lifestyle that filled my hours is becoming more distant with each passing day. I desperately want to hold on to these memories, but I know as time passes, they will fade from my memory and my life will once again be consumed with my world here. Our lives are so different. Mine complicated. Theirs so simple. Yet I feel a kinship with the Nomatzie people, a sense that maybe our fates are closely knit together. I cannot explain it.

This week I received an e-mail that upset me. Someone reportedly had spoken unkind words about me. Initially, I became angry and then defensive. My life seemed to be a house of cards, ready to fall in the slightest breeze. Later, I became despondent, wanting to give everything up for a fresh start somewhere else. My life was seemingly propelled forward toward an unknown and undesired destination by forces out of my control and contrary to my desire.

This morning I awoke early, my wife still sleeping beside me. I made coffee and brought it to her in bed. I kissed her forehead to awaken her. Smiling, she arose, sipped the hot coffee, ready to begin morning prayers. I laid down and put my head on her lap. Instinctively, she ran her fingers through my hair. I felt comforted, loved, at home and at peace. There is no safer or better place to be than here, in the arms of the one who loves you.

My wife is my closest friend. Her love is unconditional. Not because of what I do, but in spite of what I do. Yet I know that the love she has for me was given to her as a gift. It was given to her by the Author of all love, a gift from our heavenly Father. A gift to us. A good gift to enjoy and to cherish. Without Him, our love would be impossible. I am comforted by her presence. Her love surrounds me, His love flows through her. Yet, it is as if the Father of all life is gently comforting me, loving me. In this moment, nothing else seems important.

It is hard to comprehend that sometimes He chooses to love others through us. We are privileged to be His hands and His feet, an extension of His heart and His Spirit. Last week I gave myself to the Father. I prayed that He would use me in Peru, to be filled with His Spirit, His grace and His love. My heart, His heart. I used my hands to touch some gentle, lovely people far away in a distant lonely place. Did God touch them through me? Did He use my hands as His hands? Did His Spirit and grace flow through me as just now His Spirit comforts me through Sharon? I can never know. But I do know that in this moment I have all I need. There is a woman who loves me beyond all human comprehension and the God of all creation comforts me as I lie on her lap. Perhaps this is the mystery of God's love.

The Bride

S urely the presence of the Lord is in this place, I can feel His mighty power and His grace. I can hear the rush of angels' wings; I see glory on each face. Surely the presence of the Lord is in this place."[1] Hands lift in worship. Eyes gaze toward heaven, searching for the glory of God in the face of Jesus. Hearts overflow with love. Music plays softly on a keyboard, words of the praise song projected onto a wall. All brothers and sisters in Christ, for the moment, lost in wonder, love and praise.

Hot, humid, Sunday-morning air greeted me through the open window of the small church. I could see the street outside, passersby busy with life and indifferent to the worship inside. A concrete promenade, a mud bank, then the mighty Amazon River. The river flowed by, evidently no more anxious than I to rush on this sultry morning. Debris and banana leaves floated slowly past. The sprawling slum of Belén lay just yards from the sanctuary. 50,000 people crammed into a watery sewer squeezed between the banks of the Amazon and the promenade of the city of Iquitos. Mid-morning slum-life was clearly visible from where I stood, a cesspool of suffering and misery.

I had walked through the Belén market the day before. Climbing ancient stairs, I had entered by a small, dirt path, stepping into the putrefying throat of the immense garbage dump. Men and women, placed there by fate or by providence, existed a universe away from my world. The smell of rotting fish and refuse I found oppressive beyond tolerance. The crowd lightly pushed, shoulder-to-shoulder, a gentle tide of humanity surging between stalls of dried fish, spices, goat heads, and fresh meat. Several hundred people rummaged through a table of used clothes, filthy from a thousand muddy hands. Goat entrails hung from a nail above me. A young girl squatted to relieve herself on the path. She pulled her dress above her waist, her private areas plainly visible to anyone who chose to watch. But curiously, no one watched. No shame, no embarrassment, no alternative. And for a moment, countless eyes diverted, permitting an instant of privacy. Perhaps a shared accommodation, a simple, unexpected gift. Collective decency in a slum offering no respect for human existence.

Mounting the steps, I unexpectedly stood face-to-face with a middle-aged woman blocking the path in front of me. She would have been in her mid-forties. She was dressed in a dirty, white, woven, plastic flour sack with holes cut for the arms and neck. The red advertising letters around the hem proclaimed the flour brand. The sack minimally covered her body, exposing her thin legs at the mid-upper thigh. Her black, tangled and twisted hair, was matted to her head. Her face bore the pockmarks of sores from the bites of a hundred mosquitoes. Her broad, bare, calloused feet, looked excessively large in comparison to her skinny legs, almost like shoes too big. A half-naked, middle-aged harlot, standing on a little mound of fresh garbage in the middle of one of the worst slums in the world. The absolute bottom of the food chain of humanity. Selling her diseased body to any man with a few pesos, not quite the cost of a Coca Cola.

Thousands of years ago, God commanded one of his prophets to marry just such a woman. An immoral woman, impure, selfish, drunken and full of deceit. Hideous in the flesh. Not surprisingly, she would prove to be an unfaithful wife. For sale to anyone with a few coins. Yet Hosea committed his life to her and redeemed her from her many adulterous affairs. Choosing her, and only her, for his bride from all the daughters of the nations. Giving her what no one else was willing to give, his life and his unconditional love.

On the wings of the hot, humid air, the sweet sound of the praise chorus carried me back, through the window and into the sanctuary of the little church on the banks of the Amazon. The congregation still lost in praise, oblivious to my mental detour through the adjacent slums. Unaware of the beggar woman, whom I had met yesterday only yards from the sanctuary. The church, the beautiful Bride of Christ. Pure and holy, presented without spot or blemish. Greatly loved, redeemed by the blood of the Bridegroom. The Bride, destined before the foundations of the world to be resplendent in her beauty at the marriage feast of the Lamb. Arrangements perfect and complete. And all creation, from eternity past until now, waits in anxious anticipation for the revealing of the bride.

The church, the beloved, the betrothed, as filthy and as unfaithful as Hosea's wife and the harlot of Belén. The church, hideous in her sin, standing on the garbage dump of deceit, pride and division. Waiting for the bridegroom, the bride adorned in a white, plastic flour sack. Her hair dirty and matted, feet cracked and muddy, face covered in sores. Fleeing from the unconditional love of the bridegroom. Selling herself to anyone for anything. The church, who could love her? And who would choose her from among all the peoples of the earth to be His bride, His only bride?

Yet this is the beloved bride of the Son. Transformed by the unconditional love of the bridegroom. And that which the Son loves—can we love any less? "Surely the presence of the Lord is in this place, I can feel His mighty power and His grace. I can hear the rush of angels' wings; I see glory on each face. Surely the presence of the Lord is in this place."[1] In Christ, the harlot becomes a virgin again. The Church, the Bride awaits. The Spirit and the Bride say, "Come." Come swiftly, Lord Jesus.

---

[1] *Surely the Presence*, Copyright 1977, Lanny Wolfe Music

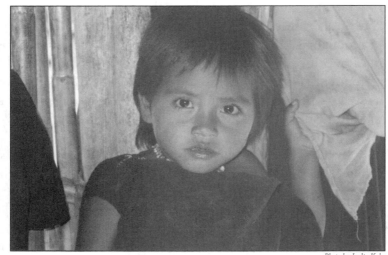

Photo by Lydia Kuhn

Nomatzieguenga Child, Amazon Jungle

New Wine

H e came to tell me about his dream—a Presbyterian minister, a Bible expositor, a man of God, my mentor and my friend. Troubled by thoughts that had come to him in the night. I have hidden his dream in my heart for more than twenty years.

He had seen a vast crowd of people standing in front of a great hall. There were immense doors. People outside, standing, waiting. They waited not in fear, and not in anxious anticipation. They just waited. Perplexed, not quite certain whether to enter.

My friend walked through the crowd to the gigantic doors. They opened without a push. He entered a great banqueting hall. There were people of all colors and all nations. People celebrating, laughing. People rejoicing. There were long tables with enormous bowls on each table. People crowded around the bowls. They all held goblets in their hands and filled them from great bowls.

Some held the filled goblets and just sniffed the aroma and smiled. Others daintily touched the liquid to their lips and laughed in glee. Others drank small sips, eyes sparkling. Others drank deeply. Still others took their goblets and joyfully gulped the drink, filling their goblets time and again from the great bowls. Aah!

Goblet in hand, at first he sniffed. The aroma was sweet. A small taste—even better. A long drink—satisfying. Then large gulps until the precious fluid ran down his lips onto his shirt. He filled his goblet time and time again. Between draughts, he threw back his head, laughing, rejoicing. It was new wine. It was satisfying. It was free. It was good.

It was the new wine of God's Spirit. And it was Jesus' blood poured out as a libation, an offering, and a sacrifice. The fragrance was the knowledge of Him. Offered freely, without limit to anyone who wished to drink. Full of grace, goodness and life.

Yet, what troubled him most were the people waiting outside. People unsure if they would enter. Didn't the great doors yield without a push? Wasn't everyone who entered rejoicing? Wasn't the new wine good, free, and sufficient for all? And why were some that entered satisfied only to sniff the new wine? And why were some satisfied with just a small drop on their lips when others would drink eagerly to their fill?

I remember so long ago the night we sat dreaming the dream together, wondering why some would refuse the banqueting feast. Wondering why everyone would not drink eagerly, deeply. It was one of the last times I saw my friend. And when I remember, I remember him drinking deeply. Drinking deeply of the new wine of God's precious Spirit. I can see him still. Laughing, rejoicing, loved. Head tilted back, the new wine dripping from his lips onto his white, starched shirt. "It is like precious oil poured on the head, running down on the beard, running down on Aaron's beard, down upon the collar of his robes. It is as if the dew of Hermon were falling on Mount Zion. For there the Lord bestows his blessing, even life forevermore."[1]

---

[1] Psalm 133:2–3 NIV

Miriam

**Michelangelo (1475–1564). Pietà, 1498-99. Marble.
St. Peter's Basilica, Vatican State.**

CREDIT: Scala / Art Resource, NY. Used by permission.

The Pietà

A s a young man, I stood in line with the rest, shuffling forward inch by inch toward a distant concrete building. Wondering why I was there, uncertain what to expect. I had come to New York for the 1964 World's Fair. Perhaps for curiosity, perhaps just to say I was there. I wanted to see Yankee Stadium. But everyone said I had to see the Pietà. It was reported to be one of the world's greatest art masterpieces. This was to be its first and only showing in the United States. So I waited—hot, tired, moving imperceptibly forward. When I finally entered the building there was some pushing. The woman behind me had her arms on my back and her gentle pressure told me that time was short. I became aware that I would have to look briefly and move on.

Suddenly, there it was. White carrara marble bathed in a peculiar jade floodlight behind a metal and plexiglas barrier. Jesus lying across the lap of the seated Mary, his arms askew, head cocked back, looking with unseeing eyes away from her in death. Mary sat motionless, head tilted down, gazing onto the lifeless body of Jesus. Inert stone, somehow alive with passion and peace. Sorrow and hope captured forever in marble. I passed by after my long wait and, until last night, the brief encounter with the Pietà slipped from my mind and heart for the next thirty-six years.

Last night in that quiet moment just between sleep and awakening, I revisited the World's Fair. There I was again, as a young man waiting in line, waiting to see the Pietà. I shuffled in with the rest. But instead of Mary, there was Jesus seated holding a middle-aged man on his lap. The man's arms were spread outward and his head cocked back just as Jesus' had been those many years before. Jesus, instead of Mary, looked lovingly into the dead man's face, his arms wrapped round the listless body. Suddenly, there was slight movement. The sculpture came alive. I realized that the man was not dead, but just resting. Resting in the lap of Jesus. I looked closer as the man adjusted his head in the crook of Jesus' arm. He was middle-aged with mostly blond hair speckled with streaks of gray. He had a full gray beard and his lips were pursed revealing a slight smile. He took a long slow breath and peacefully sighed. He looked strangely familiar. There was no pushing and I stood watching a long time, a sculpture of stone now a living drama in flesh. One of the watchers said, "Do you not recognize this man?"

"No," I replied, "but he looks familiar."

"It is you," he said, "resting in the arms of Jesus. Your struggle ended and you have come home. Jesus bears your struggles as you continue to rest in His arms."

Years before, the young man had stood silently in thought. He had grinned, then walked out of the building into the sunlight, looking for the signs to Yankee Stadium.

The Mango Tree

⁓

The Sunday sun was nearing midway in the spring sky. A canvas tarp was attached to the trees above to block the sun's direct rays. Nearly a hundred people crowded shoulder to shoulder under the tarp. The temperature was rising in the little makeshift church. Charles began his sermon. The melodious Creole was an offering to the ears. Creole to English, and then Creole again. I strained to understand the words. Undoubtedly, an excellent sermon, yet something lost in the translation. My eyes drifted from one person to another. There were small beads of sweat forming on the forehead of a pretty young girl in a spotless white nylon dress to my right. She had a red bow in her hair and her thin body and black skin were a stark contrast to her white dress. The little girl with the big brown eyes, who had been watching me, lay asleep on her mother's lap, no longer interested in the stranger beside her. Several men nodded and said "Amen." An older woman sitting at the front smiled approvingly. My eyes drifted from inside the little open-air church to a tree just outside. A mango tree. Thousands of almost-ripe mangoes hung suspended from their stems. Many showed a telltale yellow spot signaling they would soon be ripe; their juicy yellow pulp sweeter than even the best Georgia peach. And I remembered . . .

I remembered several weeks earlier I had tasted my first mango pie. It was on another Sunday. The sun had also been hot that day and sweat had soaked through my shirt. We had begun with familiar praise choruses and then I had strained to understand as Marcello preached. Tegalic, melodious as it rolled from his tongue. Tegalic to English and then Tegalic again. That day there had been another young girl in a clean white dress gently fanning away the heat. Her brown skin a contrast to her white dress. There had been a child on her mother's lap sitting beside me, staring intently until sleep finally overcame her, secure in her mother's arms.

And then I remembered another Sunday morning when Rick preached from Revelation. He spoke about peoples from every nation and every tribe crying, "Hallelujah, For the Lord our God, the Almighty reigns."[1] The mid-morning Amazon sun had flooded beneath the thatched roof into our little makeshift church. I had sat cross-legged and stared into the dense jungle hills, Nomatzieguenga tribal people surrounding me. We sang "Make Me a Sanctuary," and the jungle stood silent. There had been a pretty young woman, barefoot, wearing a brown kushma. She had pinned green parrot feathers to her shoulder for decoration—to dress in her best. There had been red paint on her brown face and a naked, sleeping, sweat-drenched child on her hip. Mangoes had been presented to us as a precious gift for visiting strangers.

With an inward smile I recalled how Osbaldo had rapidly switched back and forth between Spanish and English for the sake of the mixed congregation. Everyone in the little church had laughed when he became confused and could not remember which language he was preaching in. That day hymns had been sung in Spanish with familiar English tunes. There had been "Amens" from the men and women in the little church in the Aguan valley. And a child asleep in her mother's arms. And a pretty young woman in a clean white dress with beads of sweat on her forehead. We had all eaten a fellowship lunch together. Desert had been a delicious yellow fruit.

And then I remembered a small thatched hut, a makeshift church near my home. I had often preached there in Bengali. There had been sleeping, naked children in parents' arms and pretty young girls in clean bright saris with thin brown faces and beads of sweat on their foreheads. My hymnbook, "Cristo Songit" had become tattered and worn over the years. There had been a beautiful mango tree growing near one side of the church. I watched the mangoes grow as I passed by each day, mentally calculating the days until they would be ripe. The tree provided shade and sweet fruit for our little church as we shared our fellowship meals together.

Many thousands of miles separate us. Yet seemingly the same tarps and thatch block the Sunday morning sun. Messages of encouragement translated so all can understand. "Amens" from the congregation. Nearly naked children securely held in the loving arms of their parents. Pretty young women with brown and black faces dressed in white. All my brothers and sisters. Hot mornings, generous hearts, hymns of praise, a delicious yellow fruit and . . . unimaginable poverty. Thin, barefoot and naked, some sick and some hungry. Haiti, the slums of Manila, tribes in the Amazon, a jungle valley in Honduras, and a rural village in Bangladesh. Places of little account to the rulers of this world. Yet places and faces forever resplendent in the light of God's presence.

> How beautiful the radiant bride, who waits for her groom with
> His light in her eyes;
> How beautiful when humble hearts give the fruit of pure life
> so that others may live;
> How beautiful, how beautiful, how beautiful,
> is the Body of Christ.

> How beautiful the feet that bring, the sound of good news
> and the love of the King;
> How beautiful the hands that serve, the wine and the
> bread and the sons of the earth;
> How beautiful, how beautiful, how beautiful,
> is the Body of Christ.[2]

One day they will be there. The brown and black faces mixed with the white. Eyes that are round and dark, and some that are blue and green. The dresses, the kushmas, and the saris will be made of fine linen, bright and pure. Covenant children, and the parents who held them in their arms, singing the song of the Lamb. And there will be no translators, for we will worship with one voice and one heart singing, "Hallelujah, the Almighty reigns."

Will I recognize the pretty, young girl with a white dress and red bow in her hair? Or the naked baby in the arms of her mother? The barefoot woman with the kushma and parrot feathers? Will I recognize them in the reflection of the eyes of the bridegroom? Will I recognize them hidden in the holiness of the Lord? And mercy will flow from God, unworthy as we are. And we shall dwell together in His presence, joy unspeakable. And there will be a river, flowing from the throne of God. And a tree that yields its fruit. And the leaves are for the healing of nations. And the fruit will be sweeter than even the best Georgia peach. And there we shall feast on the fruit together, those who served and those who came to serve, the Body of Christ in the presence of the Almighty King.

---

1 Revelation 19:6b RSV
2 "How Beautiful", Twila Paris, Published by Hal Leonard

To order additional copies of

My Eyes,
His Heart

Have your credit card ready and call
Toll free: (877) 421-READ (7323)
or send $10.00* each plus $4.95 S&H** to

WinePress Publishing
PO Box 428
Enumclaw, WA 98022

or order online at: www.winepresspub.com

*WA residents, add 8.4% sales tax
**add $1.50 S&H for each additional book ordered

For more information about
Mission to the World
or participating in a short-term mission trip
please contact us or visit our web site.

Mission to the World (Presbyterian Church in America)
1600 North Brown Road
Lawrenceville, GA 30043-8141
phone: 678 823 0004
email: info@mtw.org
www.mtw.org

Photo by Lydia K

Tree at Sunset